MDN

D1356132

C333392389

In the Fast Lane!

DIXIE O'DAY: IN THE FAST LANE

A BODLEY HEAD BOOK 978 1 782 30012 0

Published in Great Britain by The Bodley Head,
an imprint of Random House Children's Publishers UK
A Random House Group Company

This edition published 2013

10 9 8 7 6 5 4 3 2 1

Text copyright © Shirley Hughes, 2013
Illustrations copyright © Clara Vulliamy, 2013

The right of Shirley Hughes and Clara Vulliamy to be identified as the author and
illustrator of this work has been asserted in accordance with the Copyright, Designs
and Patents Act 1988.

The Random House Group Limited supports the Forest Stewardship Council®
(FSC®), the leading international forest-certification organisation. Our books carrying
the FSC label are printed on FSC®-certified paper. FSC is the only forest-certification
scheme supported by the leading environmental organisations, including Greenpeace.
Our paper procurement policy can be found at www.randomhouse.co.uk/environment.

MIX
Paper from
responsible sources
FSC® C020056

RANDOM HOUSE CHILDREN'S PUBLISHERS UK
61–63 Uxbridge Road, London W5 5SA
www.randomhousechildrens.co.uk   www.randomhouse.co.uk

Addresses for companies within The Random House Group Limited can be found at:
www.randomhouse.co.uk/offices.htm
THE RANDOM HOUSE GROUP Limited Reg. No. 954009
A CIP catalogue record for this book is available from the British Library
Printed in China

In the Fast Lane!

Written by
Shirley Hughes

Illustrated by
Clara Vulliamy

THE BODLEY HEAD
LONDON

for Clara,
with
love
from
Shirley

for Mum,
with
love
from
Clara.

Contents

. . . and lots more for you to find!

INTRODUCING DIXIE O'DAY

Dixie O'Day is always ready for adventure, and he never says no to a challenge. He's the free-wheeling, car-racing hero of our story, so we caught up with Dixie at his home to see if he would answer a few questions for us . . .

Hello, Dixie! First, an easy question. What is your favourite colour?

Hello. Favourite colour? That would be red, like my car.

And what's your favourite biscuit?

I like a custard cream, but Percy prefers a Jammie Dodger.

What is your most precious possession?

My car!

Oh, of course! Can you describe your perfect day out for us?

A day out motoring with my friend, Percy. We pack a picnic and head for the seaside.

Sounds lovely! What is your most extravagant purchase?

Once I bought 54 bow ties! They were on special offer, though.

And now tell us about your ideal evening?

Well, I think it would have to be sitting by the fire, with Percy. We'd be watching a cookery programme on the television, and we'd have our supper on a tray.

What's your most embarrassing moment?
Oh dear, I'm not sure I want to tell you. Well, if I must, it would be the time my next-door neighbour, Lou Ella, saw me doing my morning exercises in my underpants.

Whoops! And finally, tell us a joke.
What do you get if you cross a dog and a daisy?
A cauliflower!
(A collie-flower, you see.)

Ha! Wonderful – thank you, Dixie, for answering all our questions, and for introducing us to you, and your friend Percy too!

Lou Ella
likes:
pink
fast cars
ice-cream sundaes

The
Friendly Family
likes:
holidays
sweets
giving a helping hand

Ron Barrakan
Owns the petrol station
and diner
Brother of Don

Don Barrakan
Owns the car repair shop
Brother of Ron

Auntie Dot
Busy with her
tomato plants
Auntie of the Friendly Dad

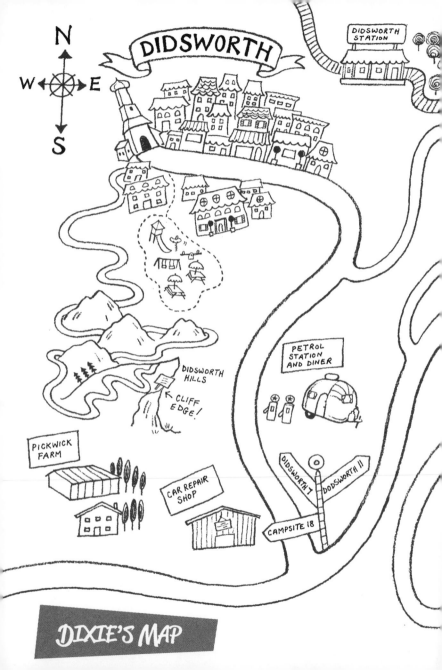

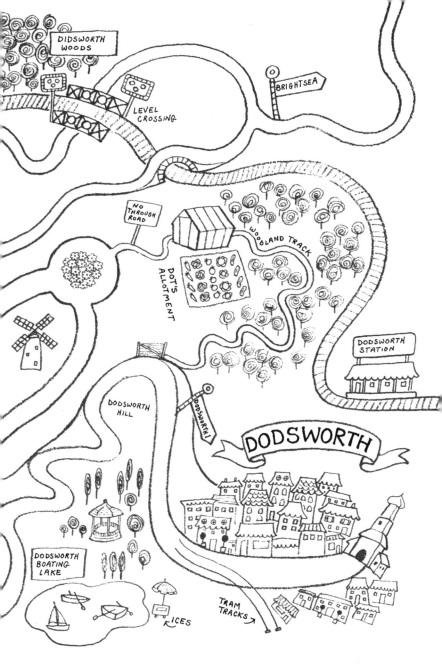

Chapter One

DIXIE O'DAY

Dixie O'Day loved his car, and took great care of it. The car was not new but it was a very clean machine. His friend Percy often came round to help him polish the bodywork until it shone.

DIXIE O'DAY

Dixie's neighbour, Lou Ella, bought a new car every year, always a very expensive one. It annoyed Dixie a lot when she drove past his house and tooted her horn.

toot!
toot!

4

Dixie often took Percy for a day in
the country. Dixie drove and Percy
admired the view.

DIXIE O'DAY

One day they took a road which led up a steep hill with hairpin bends. Halfway up, the car started to make funny noises.

thwonk!

Clunk!

Splutter!

DIXIE O'DAY

Just then, who should smoothly overtake them but Lou Ella in her brand-new pink convertible.

She pulled up a little way ahead and called out:

'You seem to be in trouble! Sorry
I can't help. It's just that I know
nothing about engines – silly old me!'
Then she waved and drove on.

DIXIE O'DAY

Black smoke was now coming out of the back of Dixie's car. Then it began to slide slowly backwards.

Dixie put on the brake but it wouldn't stop.

'We're going the wrong way!' said Percy.

'Yes, I can see that,' replied Dixie rather crossly. He was busy trying to steer, backwards. The car slid faster and faster, spun round, and they found themselves facing down the hill.

DiXiE O'DAY

The car sped on, reaching a bend
where there was a steep cliff. They
careered off the road, broke through
the railings and went right to
the edge where . . .

12

oh
phew!
the car stopped.

DIXIE O'DAY

They were halfway over a sheer drop. Percy looked down, then covered his eyes.

'We'd better get out,' said Dixie. But when they tried to move, the car wobbled.

'It might help if you could climb over into the back seat, Percy,' said Dixie.

Percy did, but he was not heavy enough to make much difference.

Dixie dared not get out of the car and push it back onto the road, because every time he tried to open the door the car slipped a little further over the edge.

They both sat there for a long time.
'I'm hungry,' said Percy. 'I wish
we'd brought a picnic.'

Dixie was hungry too, but he tried
to be brave.

In the Fast Lane!

At last a car came round the bend
and stopped.

It was a friendly family – Mum,
Dad and three little ones in the back.

DiXiE O'DAY

Dad hopped out at once to help. He tied a tow-rope to the back of Dixie's car, and the whole family heaved and lugged until slowly, slowly, they managed to pull it back onto the road.

All the little ones cheered.

'You are a true gentleman,' said
Dixie, shaking Dad's hand as they
said goodbye.

DiXiE O'DAY

It was a long walk home.

Lou Ella was standing at her gate as they trudged up the road.

'Oh dear, have you had a breakdown?' she said. 'It's really time you got a new car, Dixie.'

Dixie did not answer. He and Percy just walked into the house and shut the door.

Chapter Two

One day soon after this, a very
exciting notice appeared in town:

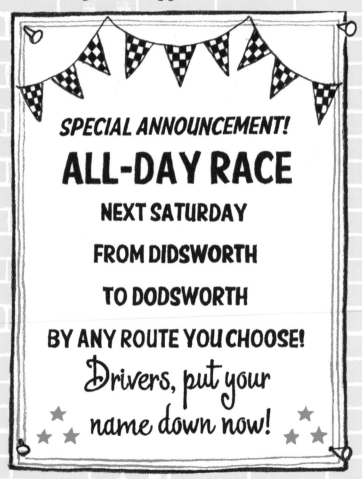

SPECIAL ANNOUNCEMENT!

ALL-DAY RACE

NEXT SATURDAY

FROM DIDSWORTH

TO DODSWORTH

BY ANY ROUTE YOU CHOOSE!

Drivers, put your
name down now!

In the Fast Lane!

'How lucky my car has been mended!' said Dixie. 'It's as good as new – well, almost – so I can join the race!'

'Can I be your co-driver?' asked Percy.

'Certainly, Percy. But I will do the driving.'

DIXIE O'DAY

When the big day came, a great
many cars were lined up at the
start. Lou Ella was there, wearing a
specially designed motoring hat.

STAR

DIXIE O'DAY

When the starting flag went down, she zoomed off ahead of everyone in a cloud of dust.

In the Fast Lane!

Dixie's car chugged along nicely.
Percy read the map.

Sometimes other drivers overtook
them . . .

and tooted their horns.

In the Fast Lane!

'Do you think you could drive a bit faster, Dixie?' said Percy, after a while.

'This is as fast as she'll go,' answered Dixie crossly. More and more cars seemed to be overtaking them. 'Let's try this side road,' said Percy, pointing to the map. 'It looks like a short cut.'

They turned off and tootled along happily.

DIDSWORTH WOODS

DIXIE O'DAY

'This is more like it,' said Dixie. 'I'm sure we're making good time now.'

Just then they came to a level crossing. The warning light was telling them STOP!

In the Fast Lane!

The gates were beginning to close. Dixie drove faster.

They were halfway across when the car suddenly stalled. Then it stopped. The wheels churned round and round. They were stuck on the railway track!

DiXiE O'DAY

The gates were nearly closed. They
could hear the train coming round
the bend.

In the Fast Lane!

Dixie jammed his foot down hard
on the accelerator.

DiXiE O'DAY

The car gave a great jolt and shot a few feet backwards. Then it shot forwards. They scraped through just as the gates clanged shut behind them.

Dixie pulled up. They sat there, breathless, listening to the train roar through.

'Perhaps this short cut isn't such a good idea after all,' said Percy.

Chapter Three

Meanwhile, Lou Ella was cruising along at high speed ahead of everyone else. She was doing so well that when she saw a notice that read:

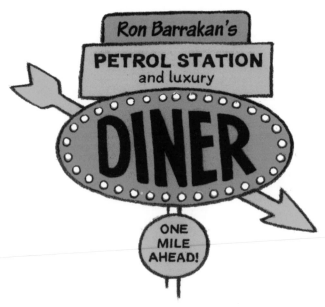

Ron Barrakan's
PETROL STATION
and luxury
DINER
ONE MILE AHEAD!

she thought she would stop and treat herself to a good lunch.

In the Fast Lane!

Ron Barrakan was standing by the petrol pumps as she drew up.

DIXIE O'DAY

'Fill up my tank and give the car a thorough clean,' she said, tossing him her car keys.

'I am well ahead in the Big Didsworth to Dodsworth Race and I want the car to look good when I come in first!'

'Certainly, madam,' Ron replied.
But there was a difficulty, because
he was not only the sole owner of the
garage, but the car-wash attendant,
chef and waiter all rolled into one.

He ran round to the back of
the diner and changed into a spotless
white apron to take her order.

Lou Ella was too busy studying
the menu to notice that it was the
same person.

Ron arranged the food carefully
on the plate and set it before her with
a flourish. Then he sprinted back to
wash and polish her car. Halfway
through he had to break off and run
back to serve her dessert.

DIXIE O'DAY

He only just had time to give the car a final wipe when he heard her calling impatiently for her bill.

'This is far too expensive!' she said when she saw it. 'The food here is horrible and the service was far too slow!'

Then she flung down only half
the money, jumped into her car and
drove off, leaving no tip.

Ron was annoyed because he reckoned he had done his best. He rang up his brother Don, who lived further up the road, and told him all about it. Don was even more annoyed.

Don had a car repair shop. Over the door it said:

DON BARRAKAN
EXHAUSTS
AND
TYRES

Nearby was a signpost that pointed the way to Dodsworth. Don was so cross that he went straight out and turned the sign in the opposite direction.

DIDSWORTH 7

CAMPSITE 18

DODSWORTH 11

DiXiE O'DAY

Minutes later Lou Ella swept past and zoomed off at great speed, going the wrong way. Then Don turned the sign back again, smiling triumphantly.

Chapter Four

DIXIE O'DAY

Dixie and Percy were now on the main road.

'I'm afraid we've lost a bit of time,' said Dixie. Cars of all sizes were speeding along, some recklessly overtaking. Dixie drove carefully, as always. He noticed a car that had broken down at the side of the road.

lollies · ices · drinks ·

18

DIXIE O'DAY

Steam was coming out of the open bonnet. None of the drivers would stop to help.

Dixie pulled in at once.
'In trouble?' he asked.

The car owner turned out to be none other than the driver who had helped them when they were stuck on the cliff edge. Now, Mum was upset and the three little ones were crying in the back.

'We're not in the race. We're just trying to get home,' said Dad gloomily.

DIXIE O'DAY

'Don't worry – it's *our* turn to help *you*!' answered Dixie.

54

In the Fast Lane!

Together they fixed up a tow-rope while Percy found some sweets for the children.

55

DIXIE O'DAY

'How can I thank you?' said Dad, when Dixie had towed them to Don Barrakan's car repair shop. 'I'm afraid we've ruined your chances in the race. But if you turn left at the next roundabout and then follow the sign where it says:

NO THROUGH ROAD

In the Fast Lane!

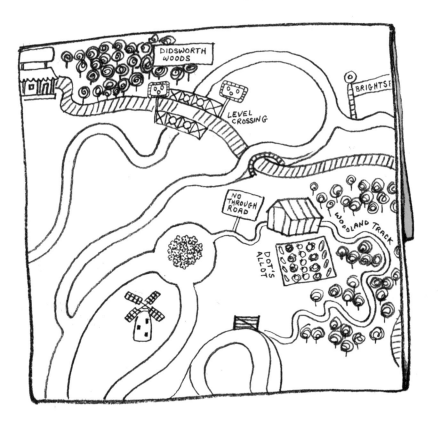

you will come to my Auntie Dot's
allotment and she may be able to help
you.'

Percy was doubtful as they drove off, but Dixie said, 'Why not? We've got nothing to lose now!'

Chapter Five

Meanwhile Lou Ella had gone a long way down the wrong road before she realized her mistake. She screeched to a halt, made a dangerous U-turn and began to speed back. She had not gone far before she ran smack into the back of a big farm truck full of sheep.

DIXIE O'DAY

The back doors flew open and the sheep came out, baa-ing joyously.

They spread in different directions all over the road.

Lou Ella tooted her horn impatiently.

'Get those silly creatures
out of the way, can't you?'
she shouted at the
farmer.

'It's your fault!' he shouted back.
'You were going too fast!'

Lou Ella's car was surrounded.
There was nothing she could do.

In the Fast Lane!

It took the farmer

a very

long time

to get all the sheep

back into the truck.

DIXIE O'DAY

By this time Dixie and Percy had found the turning signed NO THROUGH ROAD and bumped up the track. Dot was watering her tomato plants.

'Friends of my nephew? Of course I'll help you,' she said. 'There's a little track at the back of my greenhouse which leads through a wood and comes out on the main road right at the top of Dodsworth Hill. You'll be there in no time!'

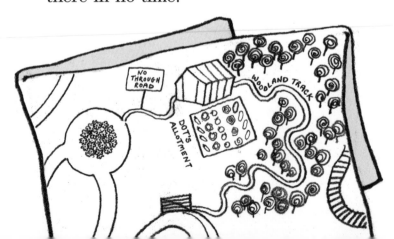

Dot's pots

It was a very bumpy track,
and when they got into the woods
Dixie had to swerve in and out of
the trees.

The car leaped and bounced.

'I hope I'm not going to be sick!' said Percy.

'No time for any of THAT,' said Dixie firmly.

At last they came to a gate at the top of the hill and Dixie jumped out to open it.

In the Fast Lane!

Below them lay the little town of Dodsworth. There was no other car in sight.

DiXiE O'DAY

"I do believe we're in the lead!" he shouted, jumping back in the car.

Chapter Six

But at that moment the engine suddenly stalled. It made a spluttering noise.

Then it stopped.

Dixie tried and tried to start it again. Nothing happened.

He got out, opened the bonnet and
looked inside.

Valuable minutes were ticking
away.

'I'll have to give her a push. You
sit in the driving seat and steer,
Percy.'

Dixie strained and pushed. The
car edged forward but still the engine
would not start. Then they heard
another car coming up behind them.
It was Lou Ella!

As she drew level with them she
slowed down and called out:

'Spot of bother? I told you to buy
a new car, Dixie. See you both in
Dodsworth after I've won!'

Then she laughed shrilly and
sped on.

At this moment Percy's car began to move forward more quickly. The engine hadn't started, but it was going downhill on its own, gathering speed as it went. Dixie only just had time to jump in and take over the steering wheel.

In the Fast Lane!

They were going faster now, but Lou Ella was still ahead. As they came near to Dodsworth, cheering crowds lined the route.

DIXIE O'DAY

'Come on, Dixie!' they shouted. 'You can do it!'

Chapter Seven

DIXIE O'DAY

Dodsworth was an old town which used to have trams, long ago. The tram lines were still there in the road.

Now, suddenly, Lou Ella found that the wheels of her car had somehow got stuck in the iron tracks.

In the Fast Lane!

'Lucky for me they're going in the right direction!' she muttered as she jammed her foot on the accelerator.

DiXiE O'DAY

In her driving mirror she could see
Dixie's car, close behind her now.

The main square was in sight. Dixie
could see the chequered flag.

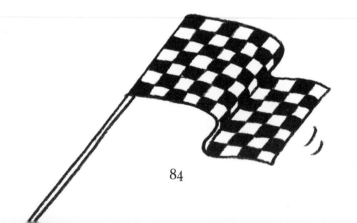

84

In the Fast Lane!

At this moment the engine of Dixie's car suddenly spluttered into life.

'SHE'S GOING!' cried Dixie.

'Come on, come on!' squeaked Percy.

Other cars were coming up
behind Lou Ella now. She was only
a short distance from the finish when,
to her horror, she realized that the
tramlines were branching off away
from the route.

She found her car being carried not towards victory but into a side street!

She tried to reverse, but it was too late. She could hear wild cheers from the crowd as Dixie and Percy passed the winning post.

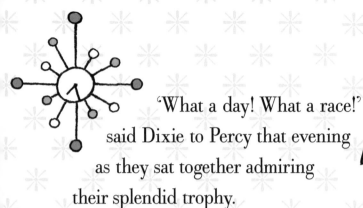

'What a day! What a race!'
said Dixie to Percy that evening
as they sat together admiring
their splendid trophy.

There was a special certificate too,
signed by the mayor of Dodsworth.

Didsworth to
Dodsworth
Race
1st place:
Dixie O'Day
& Percy!
the Mayor

Dixie
O'Day

DIXIE O'DAY

After the presentation Dixie and Percy had been carried shoulder-high by the cheering crowd.

the DODSWORTH DAILY

See page 5 for more pictures

DIXIE O'DAY IS WINNER!

The Didsworth to Dodsworth Race came to a nail-biting finish today when everyone's favourites – Dixie O'Day and his co-driver Percy – won by a whisker!

"DELIGHTED!" said Dixie.

...mayor of Dodsworth

FINISH

'It took them ever so long to get Lou
Ella's car out of the tram lines, didn't
it?' said Percy happily.

DiXiE O'DAY

'Will you get a new car now, Dixie?'
'Oh no, I don't think so. Let's give
her a good clean and take her on an
outing.'

In the Fast Lane!

As they were loading their picnic
into the boot they saw Lou Ella
standing at her gate. She was still
wearing her motoring hat and trying
to look as if nothing
had happened.

DIXIE O'DAY

'Sorry you had a spot of bother,' called Dixie. 'Better luck next time. Perhaps you'd better buy a new car?'

Lou Ella did not reply.

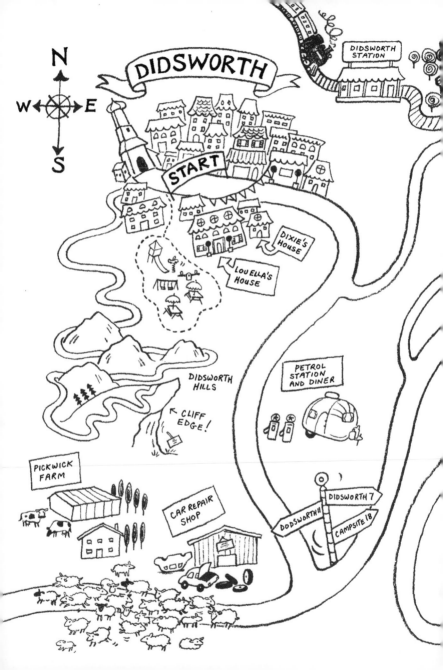

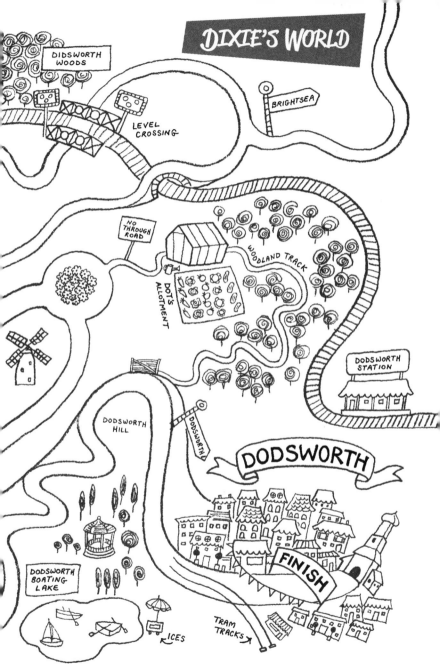

I SPY

Look out of the window (or around the car) and pick something you can see (for example, a sheep). Then say, 'I spy, with my little eye, something beginning with S' (or whichever is the first letter of the word you have picked). The other people in the car have to guess what you are thinking of: sand, sun, sweets or sandwiches!

The Number Plate Game

Pick a number plate and look at the letters in it. Can you make a word from them? For example, a number plate with BCK in it might be BACK, or BUCKLE or BUCKET!

WHO AM I?

Think of an object, animal, plant or person. The other people in the car have to guess who or what you are, by asking you questions that can only be answered with 'Yes' or 'No'. For example, 'Are you female?' 'Would I find you by the seaside?' 'Are you larger than this car?' 'Do you like custard creams?'

Tell jokes and sing songs!

Dixie and Percy know lots of (terrible) jokes, which they like to tell on car journeys. Here's one of their favourites: **What do you call a country where everyone has to drive a pink car?** *A pink car nation.* Try telling jokes with your family! Percy also likes to sing songs in the car, though Dixie isn't quite so keen. What's your favourite song to sing?

I'M GOING TO . . .

This is a memory game. One person picks somewhere for you all to go (for example, to a museum), and starts the game off by picking an object they are taking with them: 'I'm going to a museum, and I'm bringing my spectacles'. The next person repeats this, and adds something of their own: 'I'm going to a museum and I'm bringing my spectacles and my sketchpad'. Keep going, and see how many things you can remember (in the right order, of course)!

The Story Game

Make up a story together! One person starts (perhaps with 'Once upon a time . . .') and then passes the story to the next person. Let your imaginations run wild! You can always use what you see out of the window to help you.

Percy's Perfect Car Games

Dixie and Percy love going for long car rides. They pack a picnic and set off – sometimes with a map, but sometimes they just like to see where they will end up. Percy loves playing games when Dixie is driving. Above are some of his favourites:

Marvellous Motors!

Can you draw your own wonderful vehicle? Perhaps it isn't a car – maybe it is a bath with wheels or something else entirely.

Does it fly, or go in water? How many people will fit inside, and what colour will it be?

Get some paper and drawing materials and come up with your own marvellous motor.

Go to www.dixieoday.com to find out how to send your drawing to Dixie!

The Dixie O'Day Quiz

Dixie has written a special quiz to test you! How much can you remember about *Dixie O'Day In the Fast Lane?*

1. What is on Dixie's number plate?

2. How often does Lou Ella buy a new car?

3. How many children are there in the Friendly Family?

4. Where does the All-Day Race start from?

5. What colour is Lou Ella's new car?

6. Who owns the petrol station and diner?

7. And what is his brother called?

8. Lou Ella gets surrounded by which farm animal?

9. Dot is watering which plants?

10. Who wins the All-Day Race?

11. And who do you think comes second?

12. What is the name of the newspaper that Dixie and Percy appear on the front of?

My great-grandfather,
Sea Admiral Dexter Duckworth O'Day

My Aunt Daisy

Mum and Dad

me when I was two

my first go-kart

Can you spot me and Percy in our old school photograph?

AND FINALLY, introducing Shirley Hughes and Clara Vulliamy – the dashing duo behind Dixie and Percy's adventures!

Shirley Hughes

LIKES:

sketchbooks, friendly neighbours, ballroom dancing

DISLIKES:

airports, spiders, long queues

Clara Vulliamy

LIKES:

chocolate buttons, goats, motorcycles with sidecars

DISLIKES:

peas, alarm clocks, losing her glasses

Did you know that Clara is Shirley's daughter? This is the first book they have created together!

If you enjoyed

DIXIE O'DAY
In the Fast Lane,

then you'll love Dixie and Percy's

next adventure

DIXIE O'DAY
and the

Great Diamond Robbery

Read on for the first chapter . . .

DiXiE O'DAY
and the Great Diamond Robbery

Chapter One

One fine summer morning Dixie O'Day said to his friend Percy:

'I've decided that it's time to take a little holiday. Would you accompany me, Percy?'

'You bet!' said Percy. 'Shall we take the tent and go camping?'

'No, I'm thinking of something a bit more luxurious. I'm

booking us in at the Hotel Splendide at Brightsea!'

'The Hotel Splendide! That's one of the very poshest hotels on the coast! Won't it be terribly expensive?'

'Never mind that,' Dixie replied nonchalantly. 'I've been saving up for a long while now, and it's time we had a bit of a treat.'

'I'd better pack my bow tie,' Percy said.

'Oh, yes,' said Dixie. 'And of course we will have to take our dinner jackets to change into in the evening.'

'Oh dear!' said Percy. 'I only have the one which belonged to my Uncle Gus! I'm afraid it's a bit moth-eaten, and there are a couple of gravy stains . . .'

'Never mind. Give it a bit of a sponge over, Percy, and you'll look fine. Don't forget you're one of the best ballroom dancers I know – why, you've even won competitions!'

'I'll do my best not to let you down,' said Percy bravely.

They both set to work to give Dixie's car a good clean, and polished the bodywork until it shone.

It was not long before they were driving happily towards Brightsea. They had chosen a quiet side road which had more scenic views that the motorway and very little traffic.

They were cruising merrily along, when suddenly another car zoomed up behind them, seemingly out of nowhere and travelling at reckless speed. It followed closely, almost touch-ing their back bumper, then pulled out and shot past them with inches to spare. There might

Adventure and excitement await
Dixie and Percy when they arrive
at the Hotel Splendide. Percy's
favourite pop star – the glamorous
Peaches Miaow – is staying there,
but disaster strikes when her
diamond necklace is stolen.

**Will Dixie be able to solve this
dastardly crime?**

Find out in

DIXIE O'DAY
and the Great Diamond Robbery